The Words of My Father

By Mark Nemetz

Scripture is taken from the HOLY BIBLE, NEW INTERNATIONAL
VERSION®. NIV®. Copyright © 1973, 1978, 1984 by International
Bible Society. Used by permission of Zondervan. All rights reserved
worldwide.

Higher Ground Books & Media
Springfield, Ohio.
http://highergroundbooksandmedia.com

Printed in the United States of America 2020

Our Father

"Papa, do I have to go to sleep now? I'm not tired," little Joseph whined, looking up at his father with pleading eyes. "Yes, my son," Giuseppe replied, leaning down to kiss the boy on the forehead. "But why?" Joseph asked, swallowing a yawn. "Because I know my son needs his rest; today was a full day, and tomorrow will be another set of adventures, and we both want to be prepared for that, don't we?" Giuseppe asked. The boy nodded and took his father's hand. "But first, let's pray together, son," Giuseppe said. The boy nodded but then paused. "But Papa, tell me what the prayers mean. I don't understand the words." Giuseppe knew Joseph was trying to delay the moment of going to sleep, so he thought of his tactic. "All right, son, we can try to understand the words together but only one phrase this evening, one phrase tomorrow, until we reach the end." The boy smiled, happy with the arrangement.

"Which prayer do you want to say, son?" his father asked. "Let's start with the *Our Father*," Joseph said as Giuseppe nodded. "What do you want to know, son?" he asked. "Papa, why do we say, 'Our Father'? I mean, you're my father. I don't understand." Giuseppe smiled and stroked his son's hair as he sat on the bed. "I am your father, and that can help us understand who God is. Son, if He weren't like a father to us, God would be someone we would serve and obey but would be afraid of; it would be as if we would listen to what He told us because we would think, if we didn't, He would punish us. It's easier to explain if I think of my papa, your grandfather. When I think of him, I'm not afraid of him, I love him, and I know he loves me. Now I can't prove to someone else that my father loves me; I can't measure his love with a ruler or pour it into a measuring cup. It's not something that I can hold in my hand, but my father has done so many hundreds and thousands and probably millions of things for me that the only logical conclusion is that he loves me. He has shown himself to be a father to me and a grandfather to you. So, when I say that prayer, I remember how my father loves me."

"Is that enough for tonight, son?"

"Papa, Nathan in my class, doesn't have a father; he says his father left, and he can hardly remember him, and he is mad at him. Who can Nathan think about when he prays?" Joseph asked. Giuseppe paused before answering. "For some, it is more difficult. If I didn't have my papa, it might take more effort to imagine God as my Father, but then I remember how I know my father loves me. I recall that he worked all day, held me on his knee, played ball with me, and asked me about my day, that he spent time with me - all these things and more, the same is true for God. So, one who doesn't have a father has to take a greater leap, but the signs of love are still there."

"Papa, did you ever make grandpa sad?"

Giuseppe smiled. "You are not there yet, son, but there is a time when one is between being a boy and becoming a man that is difficult for the son and the father. It was probably during this time that I sometimes, without wanting to, made my father sad…" "How, Papa?" Joseph asked. "I don't want to give you any bad examples, son, but sometimes I thought I knew better, though I didn't, and sometimes I thought I was already grown up, which I wasn't. There were times when I didn't listen to my father, and I had to learn from my mistakes. But I never doubted that your grandpa loved me even when I went my own way, and I think he knew I loved him even if I didn't always listen or follow his advice. That's how a relationship is, son; we all make mistakes, we're all human, but that doesn't take away from the love. When I say *Our Father,* I don't think about all the mistakes I've made or weaknesses I have, but I think about the love I have for the Father and that He has for me. I think about the love, son."

"Are you ready to go to sleep, son?"

"Papa, what's a father?"

Giuseppe leaned back and looked at the ceiling before answering. "If I told you that it is a man who has a son, that would be too easy, and it is only part of it. When I call my papa "father," it means so much more than helping me be born. Being a father is a lifelong relationship; I will always be your father, and you will always be my son. Now, what type of father will I be for my son? That is an important question. Just being related isn't enough because fatherhood means teaching my son by my example to have integrity, strength, patience, and a heart. When I think about your grandpa, I think of integrity - I don't think he ever told a lie in his life - and love since he is an emotional person, and we were always very close, and we still are. By emotional, I mean that your grandpa has a rare gift: he can feel what other people feel. The word for this is 'empathy,' which you probably haven't learned yet (the boy shook his head), but it means that someone can rejoice with those who rejoice and suffer with those who suffer. I remember when I was a bit older than you, I came home from school one day sad because I learned that a friend of mine, who was in class with me, had died in a car accident. My father saw that something wasn't right, but I didn't want to talk about it. So, he just sat with me and chatted about his day until I was ready. I told him the story of my friendship with this boy and how we said we would go to the same college and that we would always be friends, but then he was gone. When I looked up at my father, he was crying as he was listening. Then I knew that he understood, and I saw part of your grandpa that I never saw before, and I thought 'I want to be like him.' So being a father doesn't just mean being related; it means having a relationship of love with your son. It means showing your son how to live in the world with heart and integrity and knowing that the love that binds you is stronger than any mistake you could make. Does that make sense, son?" Giuseppe asked. The boy nodded.

"But Papa," Joseph continued, "how can I think of all this when I say *Our Father?*" Giuseppe chuckled. "Well, son, you don't. Just think of one thing when you say that word 'Father;' if you can relate the words to something you experience, it can mean more." "But Papa," the boy continued, "Does that mean that when I say the 'Our Father' I should think of you?" Giuseppe laughed again. "Let me tell you a story, son. When I was your age, I thought my father was perfect and that everything he said was right and that he could tell the future. So, if my father would say 'it will rain tomorrow,' I was sure it would. I laugh at this now, but when I was small, it seemed like my dad was the best and didn't have any faults and knew all this stuff that nobody else knew. But as I grew up, I realized that my dad wasn't perfect; I don't want to get into details but, to make a long story short, I realized that he was human. But when I think of the Father in heaven, I think of Him, not as a human but somehow free of all the faults that hold us back. So, my father on earth helps me begin to imagine my Father in heaven, but at a certain point, that doesn't work anymore, because the Father in heaven is greater. So, I don't think of my papa as my heavenly Father; I just think of him as my dad who was given to me by my heavenly Father, and I think I was pretty lucky," Giuseppe concluded.

"So, I think that I have said everything I have to say about what the first part of that prayer means for me. Are you ready to sleep, son?" Joseph shook his head. "But Papa, you forgot part of it! You forgot the 'our' part. Why is it 'our' Father, Papa? I mean, you're *my* father, not our father…," Giuseppe laughed; "I don't think your sister would agree with that, son!" Joseph laughed also. "But Papa, why can't I say, 'My Father' instead of 'Our Father?' I mean, if I introduce you to my friends at school, I say that you are 'my father' Papa, I don't say 'this is our father'!" "Well, let's think about that, my son. If we are at your school and your sister is there, would you say 'my' or 'our' father? Do you see what I mean, son? When you say 'our father,' it means that you and your sister Emma are related, that there is not only a bond between you and me, but a bond between you and her, because you have the same father. So that 'our' makes a big difference in the way we see other people."

"Let me give you an example, son. Think about those homeless people living in those tents under the bridge that we see whenever we head towards downtown. Now sometimes we bring them food; you have been in the car when we have done this. Just small things: cookies, bread, hot chocolate. Why do you think we do that, son?" The boy looked at his father and answered in a tone as if he was taking an exam. "Because you feel sorry for them?" Giuseppe nodded. "That is part of it, son; I do feel sorry for them because of all the painful things that they have gone through to end up living on the streets. Yes, I do feel sorrow, but there is another reason. What do you think I am thinking about when I say *Our Father…*" "Well, Papa," the boy began; "if you say, 'our Father' it must mean that those homeless people are your brothers and sisters and that they are my brothers and sisters too." Giuseppe was nodding. "Yes, son, when I say 'Our Father,' I am saying that everyone is my brother and sister because we have the same father so that everyone is deserving of love and kindness, shelter, and food…" "But Papa!" the boy interrupted; "if it's true that they are our family, then why don't we invite them to come live with us?" Giuseppe looked in his son's eyes for a minute before answering. "That's an excellent question, son. I think it is easy to do everything or nothing but not in between. What I mean is, I cannot bring the homeless into our home because I have all of you to take care of, we don't have extra rooms and my salary wouldn't cover our expenses. But it would be easy for me to say to myself, 'I can't take them off the streets so I won't do anything for them.' It is easy to become indifferent, not to look at other people's suffering, son. Maybe I can't do everything for those homeless living a few streets over, but I can do something. So that is why, remembering that these are our brothers and sisters, your mother and I sometimes bring them food, especially when it is cold and always on the holidays. So yes, son, these are our brothers and sisters, and if I can do a little something for them, I will."

Giuseppe pointed up as he said: "So son, one word points us up, as we think of the Father in heaven who I cannot see with my eyes, and the other word points to those around us, who I can see. When I say these first two words of the prayer, I know that because I have a special relationship of love with the Father that I also have a special relationship of love with his other children. I hope that helps you say your prayer, son," Giuseppe said as he kissed his son's forehead. The boy no longer fought it, but before his father left the room, he said in a sleepy voice: "Thank you, Papa. Tomorrow you can tell me why God lives in heaven." The boy then drifted into sleep.

Who art in heaven

"Are you ready to go to sleep tonight, son, after you say your prayers? Are you tired?" Joseph shook his head. "I'll be ready to go to sleep after you tell me what heaven is and why God lives there." Giuseppe smiled and said, "I think I need to bring your mother in on this one." Rising from the bed, Giuseppe left the room and returned with his wife Helen, who sat on the boy's bed while Giuseppe stood off to the side.

"Son, I thought your mother might have more experience in this area than I do, so why don't you repeat your question." The boy took his mother's hand and asked, "Where is heaven, mom? And why does God live there?" Helen glanced up at her husband, then at her son's face, and then looked down to reflect. A full minute passed before she looked up and asked Joseph: "Do you remember your grandmother, son? You were so small when she passed away." The boy looked at the ceiling as if he saw something. "Barely; I sort of remember when she held me," he said. "Well, when my mother passed away, it was difficult since we were very close. One day she was there, and the next she was gone, and I didn't know how to think about it, but I remember how bad it made me feel. In the days and weeks after she passed away, I asked her to send me a sign that she was all right, but no sign arrived. I asked and asked, and still no sign. I didn't understand how my mother could love me and be in heaven without sending me a sign. If heaven is a faraway place, my mother should be able to get me a message. But I looked and looked for some small unexplainable miracle, and all I found was silence. So, this made me begin to wonder what heaven is. I don't know if I have an answer, but I can at least tell you what it isn't."

"I don't believe that heaven is a physical place, up in the clouds or another planet," Helen began. "If it were, then I know I would have heard from my mother by now. I would have gotten a mysterious letter; someone would have read my thoughts, or my lightbulb would begin tapping out Morse code. None of this happened. No, son, I think heaven is more like a state of being rather than a place. What I mean is that heaven is another type of existence. When I want to see you, I just come into your room or call out 'Joseph!' and there you are because we have physical bodies, so if you are back in your room, I can find you. But in heaven, it is different. I can't look for my mother as I can for you, but, over time, I understood that my mother was still with me, but differently, and that the signs I was asking for were given, but I didn't see them…"

"What sign, Mamma? Did you see a miracle?" Helen smiled. "Well, the miracle was more within me than something out there. I saw my mother's love in your face, in Emma's face, in your father's eyes, and my memories. I can feel that your grandmother is still with me, but I cannot explain how…"

"But Mamma, where is grandma? Don't say she is in heaven; tell me *where* she is!" the boy insisted.

"Well, maybe I cannot tell you *where* your grandmother is, but I can say *what* I think heaven is. I think heaven has to do with those we love; it's a place where love is purified of all its cloudiness and becomes something clear, like pond water becoming drinkable. All the selfishness is filtered out until only the love remains. And, connected with this, heaven is where God is. It is as simple as that. If someone asked me where heaven is, I would say that it is where God is. It is sort of like my mother, who was always happy and joyful, and wherever she went, she brought that joy with her. Whoever was around my mother became part of her joy; heaven is the same. Whoever is around God becomes part of that love. So, when I say those words 'Who art in heaven,' I think about that love that comes from God, like two arms reaching out, holding all those I both care about and those I don't even know. So, God is with the people that I love, and somehow, they are with Him, and since I don't ever feel He is far, so those I love aren't far away either. That is what I understand when I say, 'who art in heaven,' son."

"Are you ready to go to sleep, son?" Giuseppe asked. "Not yet, Papa. Mamma, why does God live in heaven and not here, and why did He take Grandma with Him?" Helen laughed and said, "I don't know if I have the answers to those questions, son, but I don't think that God lives in heaven, and we are stuck here as if He lives in Beverly Hills and we are in the projects. I think that God does live here, because He is the Father, just as your papa explained last night; a loving father is never far from his kids. Would we be good parents if we moved to Beverly Hills and left you and your sister on the streets to fend for yourselves? Of course not, we wouldn't do that because we love you. So, it is the same with God. When I was so sad after I lost my mother, I realized that after some days of feeling alone, I wasn't alone and that the Father was with me the entire time. I just couldn't see this because my sadness was so great. I eventually realized that your father was with me the whole time, along with you and your sister. For a while, I couldn't see this because of my grief. But when I did see that I was not alone and that I was being accompanied along this path, I felt better. Today, though I miss my mother dearly, I don't feel so sad when I think of her; instead I feel grateful. Perhaps that is the miracle that I was asking for: to feel gratitude when I remember her."

Helen looked down and saw that her son had fallen into a deep sleep. "How are you?" Giuseppe asked his wife as he looked into her tear- filled eyes. "I miss her," she replied.

Hallowed be thy name

"Papa, what does that word mean?" Giuseppe smiled at his son as he sat down on the bed. "Let's start with the easy part, son. What is a 'name'?" Joseph answered, "It is what you are called!" Giuseppe nodded. "What about a family name, like the one that I share with you and your sister, your mother, and my parents? What is that?" Joseph put his finger on his chin as he thought very hard. "It means you're my family!" he said triumphantly. Giuseppe nodded. "Yes, son! So, a name isn't just a word; a family name means you belong to a family. So, think about your grandfather; think about his first and his last name. Do you have his name in your mind? So when I was growing up, everyone at school and in my neighborhood knew that I was his son, and he was my father because we shared the same name and lived in the same house, and we were always together." Giuseppe shifted on the bed and began to use his hands as he spoke. "So, when I was at school, and if I misbehaved, this reflected on my father and mother; they would get a phone call from school if I didn't behave. If I brought home all good grades, this also reflected on them; people would say what a good job they did in raising their children. I somehow honored my father's name when I did good and dishonored it when I did bad. Does that make sense, son?" The boy nodded.

"When he was a boy, my brother, your uncle, used to get in trouble at school. Sometimes he didn't do his homework, or he would talk back to his teachers. I remember when my mother got a phone call from the school, asking her to come down and speak with the principal. An hour later, all of us, including your grandmother, your uncle, the principal, and me, were all at the school listening to the principal describe the trouble my brother had gotten into that day. I don't even remember what it was. But I do remember my mother crying in front of all of us. She didn't scold my brother; she didn't even show any anger. She just cried. My brother never misbehaved again after that."

"Now, in your case, people we know and even strangers have come up to us and said, 'What wonderful children you have; you must be great parents!' So, by being such wonderful kids, you honor our name, bring respect to our family, and make us proud of you."

"Papa!" the boy said, "We're not that wonderful.... are we?"

Giuseppe laughed. "Yes, you are, son," he replied.

"So, when we say, 'Hallowed be thy name,' we ask that God's name be hallowed or honored. Just as you honor your family name by being such a great boy, so we honor God's name if we live the way He wants us to. When I ask God that His name be honored, I am also praying for all those around me who share Him as our Father; that includes everyone, son. We have a kinship with one another that we sometimes forget, and the words of this prayer remind us to pray for each other and to help one another so we can honor the Father."

"But how do we honor his name? The first way is to recognize that we belong to one family with one Father in heaven. When we remember this, then we judge others less, and we are more gentle and forgiving. The other ways we honor His name, that we live the words of that prayer, are explained by the part that comes after. But that, son, has to wait until tomorrow," Giuseppe concluded, bending down to kiss his son's forehead.

T hy kingdom come

"Papa, what's a kingdom," Joseph asked from under his covers. Giuseppe sat at the end of his bed and asked, "What is a king, son?" The boy thought for a few moments. "A king is a man who wears a crown and sits on a throne and has lots of power and everyone serves him, and his father was the last king" was the response. Giuseppe nodded. "So, a kingdom is?" "Papa," the boy responded, "it's where the king lives!" Giuseppe paused and reflected. "Son, can there be a kingdom without a king?" Joseph responded immediately. "No Papa, a kingdom is where the king lives, so if there is no king, then there is no kingdom!" Giuseppe laughed. "Now you are teaching me, son! OK, one more question: can there be a king without a kingdom?" The boy thought and thought. "I think so, Papa. If there is a king and he doesn't have any land or anyone to serve him, then he is a king without a kingdom," Giuseppe smiled.

"I wonder, son, if God has a kingdom or not, and where this kingdom might be. After all, if I am asking that his kingdom might come, doesn't that mean that He doesn't yet have a kingdom?" The boy looked perplexed. "Son, if God were the president, He would preside over the United States; if He were the king of England, He would be king of, well, England! So, where is God's kingdom?" The boy answered hesitantly. "In heaven?" Giuseppe smiled and squeezed his son's hand. "Yes, in heaven, and maybe He wants to expand it in us too. You see, son, when I say, 'thy kingdom come,' I think of those parts of my heart where I honor him and those parts where I don't. I also think of everyone I know and those I don't know, and I pray that His kingdom might come among us, that we might recognize our kinship, having one Father, and might treat each other like a brother or sister. So for me, son, when I say 'thy kingdom come' I remember that I am no different from that man on the street; we all need help, none of us is perfect, and we ask the Father to adjust our hearts a little bit every day to make them like His. That's the kingdom that I ask for."

Joseph lay there a long time thinking, then said, "Papa, tell me a story!" Smiling, Giuseppe rubbed his son's head and began. "When I was a young boy, even younger than you, my father used to read me stories. The ones I enjoyed the most were about far off kingdoms with knights and princesses and adventures on horses. I sometimes wondered if there had been a king in our family, or I wished it. But one night, my father read me a story about a bad king who used his power to hurt others and take advantage of other people's goodness. This bad king didn't think of his subjects, but only of himself and, eventually, his kingdom turned against him. They drove him out, and his brother took over his kingdom, where he ruled in peace because he cared for his subjects. His brother was seen as a good king because, when the people ran out of water because of lack of rain, he sent his soldiers out to dig wells. Another time, when the towns needed new roads, this king didn't raise taxes but instead sold off half of his land to pay for the roads. From these and other actions, the people understood that this new king thought of his subjects before thinking of himself; they understood that this king loved his people and worked and sacrificed for their happiness. The people in other kingdoms saw this and wanted to live under this king because his kingdom was more just and merciful. So when we say 'thy kingdom come,' I also think of these childhood stories and of a kingdom that I want to belong to where everyone treats each other with love and respect, where the lives of the people matter to the king."

"Now the last thing I will tell you, son, is that 'hallowed by thy name' and 'thy kingdom come' are connected. I ask that a kingdom come in which we might honor the name of the one who loves us and who desires our happiness, just as I love you, and that we might see one another as part of one family."

"Good night, my son."

"Papa!" Joseph called out. "Yes, son?" "Where is that kingdom?" Giuseppe answered, "It is in our hearts, son. Good night."

Thy will be done on earth as it is in heaven

"Are you ready to go to sleep, son?" Giuseppe asked as Joseph pulled his blankets up to his chin. The boy shook his head, so Giuseppe sat on his son's bed. "All right, son, what is the next part of the prayer?" Joseph looked up at the ceiling as he recited the lines 'thy will be one on earth as it is in heaven.' "Do you know what that means, son?" The boy shook his head again. "Well, we are asking for something. What are we asking for here?" "I don't know, Papa," the boy responded timidly. "Well, we are asking for a lot of things in this prayer. We ask that our brothers and sisters honor His name and treat each other like family; then, we ask that His kingdom come where we feel safe and loved. So here we are asking for a third thing. What do you think that is, son?" "Hmmmmmm," the boy thought. "That what He wants to done here might be done just like it gets done in heaven." Giuseppe jumped back. "Yes, son! That is something that makes me think. Just as it gets done in heaven…" "But I still don't understand, Papa," the boy complained.

Giuseppe smiled and patted his son's hand as he thought. "There were two brothers," he began, "whose father was a king. So, if they were sons of the king, they are…." "Princes!" Joseph said. Giuseppe nodded. "When they came of age, their father, the king, gave them each a castle, identical to each other, so the brothers would not be jealous. Each castle came with the same number of cooks and gardeners and guards and knights. They even had the same number of pigs and cows!" Joseph laughed. "So the two castles were identical: the gardens were well kept and lush; the cook in each castle made wonderful meals and cakes and cookies; the cleaners made sure the floors and walls and furniture were spotless, and everyone got along. But one brother preferred to stay in the castle and on his grounds and make sure that everything was running smoothly. The other brother liked to travel, so soon he grew bored being in his castle every day. At first, he traveled for just a day, then two days, once he took a trip for a week. After a while, he began taking longer trips until he was away for an entire year traveling the world!" "Gee Papa, he's lucky!" "Yes, he was lucky, son, but what do you think was happening in a castle when he was away for so long?" The boy wondered and then asked his father, "What was happening, Papa?" "Well, the cooks, when they saw the Prince was rarely at home, stopped preparing meals. Occasionally, they did make a feast, but they invited their friends and family to eat the Prince's food. When they saw that there was no one to oversee their look, the gardeners stopped mowing the lawn and grew lazy about watering the flowers, which soon turned brown. The cleaners started neglecting the inside of the castle, and soon there was dust and ants everywhere. And the people who honored the Prince were sad because they saw that few were doing what the Prince wanted them to do had he been there."

"Now the other son of the king stayed at his castle and made sure that the cooks prepared the meals and the cakes and cookies, that the cleaners dusted every piece of furniture and mopped the floors every day and the gardeners made sure that the plants flourished. Those who lived on this Prince's estate were proud of their castle, grounds, and Prince, who took such good care of everything he had been entrusted with."

Joseph looked at his father as Giuseppe continued. "One day, this brother invited the other Prince's household over for a feast; there would be food, music, and dancing. Everyone who lived on the estate was invited, but many workers did not come because they were ashamed. But those who did come to the feast saw the difference; they saw that the house was spotless, that the garden was lush, and that the food was delicious, just as the Prince wanted it. Those from the other estate began to murmur, 'I wish our estate was like this. I wish our castle were clean, and our gardens were growing and that our kitchens produced food. I wish that those who serve the Prince would carry out his will, whether he was in the castle or not. Our Prince is a good man, but he likes to travel; I wish those who serve him loved him enough to carry out his will and not just fear his punishment." Some of those present gathered the courage to approach the brother prince who was hosting the feast; 'Honorable sir' they began, 'We are grateful for the feasting and your hospitality. One can see that your will is always done in your castle and on your estate since everything here is beautiful and harmonious. Please help us so that your brother's will might be carried out on his estate and that those who say they serve him in words may do so in deeds.' This brother, who was now growing in wisdom, looked with compassion on his brother's subjects and answered: 'My brother is lord of his estate and I hope that you share this with him. His other servants know that they do evil; for that reason, they are not here. They fear his return because they may get caught in their neglect since they do not serve him from love. But I will speak to my brother and his servants. I will implore them that his will may be done on his estate so that harmony is restored and what is neglected be set right."

"This is what 'thy will be done on earth as it is in heaven' means. In heaven, in that 'castle,' there is harmony based on love. There are none of the complications that we put between ourselves; it is where all recognize and feel that they are brothers and sisters and where the other always comes first. We ask that our castle, which is beautiful but messy, become more like that heavenly castle, which is fantastic."

"So, Papa, we have to clean God's house?" Joseph asked. Giuseppe took his son's hand and chuckled. "In a way, son, yes, but in our hearts. But I see it like this. Doing the will of the Father isn't like doing chores, but it is more about making good choices and knowing that I am never alone. I can understand this better if I think of you: if I see you sad sometimes, son, this makes me sad because what I want most for you is that you be happy. I want this so much," Giuseppe said as he squeezed his son's hand. "But if I think of my own life, I can see that being happy comes from two things: making good choices for myself and knowing that I am not alone. Let me give you an example, son. When I was a little older than you, when I was in high school, I became friends with a group of boys who always got into trouble. I wanted to be accepted, so when they didn't go to class, I didn't go; when they got into trouble, I got into trouble. I remember that I was only sixteen years old; I was so sad when my grades went down so far that my teachers called my father. I can still picture how disappointed he looked; his disappointment made me feel even worse about myself. But your grandfather, my father, rather than punishing me, asked me why I was making these choices. He asked me why I was doing what these boys wanted me to do rather than what I wanted; your grandfather had a point. I was doing their will rather than the right thing. So, I refocused myself on making good choices, I made some new friends, and I got back on the path to graduate. I realized that my sadness came from making the wrong choices. My father wished he could make the choices for me, but he knew that I was the only one who could change my path, and that is what he told me: it is my choice and my life. What he said scared me because I saw that the type of life I would have now depended on the choices I made then. So, I think, with God, it is the same. He sees our choices, and He so wishes He could step in and choose for us, but it is our life, and we have to decide what type of life we want. My father wanted me to be happy, and I think it is the same for God; I believe He wants us to make choices that will lead us closer to happiness.

"So, Papa, when I am good, then God will send me good things?" the boy asked. Giuseppe smiled. "Do you believe in Santa Claus, son?" he asked. The boy nodded. "Well, God is not Santa Claus. At Christmas, we believe that if you are good, you will get presents, but if you have been bad, you might get a piece of coal. But in life, some excellent people have bad things happen to them, and those who are very bad have good things happen. So I think, son, that when we say 'thy will be done' we are saying yes, I accept these things that are difficult for me, but I know that I am not alone, I know that the Father is my companion. Things that happen to us may make us happy sometimes or sad other times, but then I remember that the Father is my father and that He will not abandon me, just as I would never leave you, my son. When I remember this, everything difficult becomes a little more bearable, and everything happy becomes a little more joyful because I know that I am not alone."

"Are you sleepy yet, son?" The boy shook his head. "Tomorrow, you will not want to get up! Try to sleep, son," he said, as he kissed Joseph's head.

Give us this day our daily bread

"Do you have everything you need, son?" Giuseppe asked as he tucked Joseph in. "I have you; I have mom, I have my sister, we have a house, we have food, I have clothes...I think so, Papa!" the boy said. "Do you have everything you want, son?" Giuseppe continued. "Papa! You know I want a horse or a pony!" Giuseppe laughed. "Yes, I know, son. But I think that when we say 'give us this day our daily bread,' we ask for what we need rather than what we want. Do you want to think about this, son?" The boy nodded as Giuseppe sat down.

"Sometimes, we say a prayer before we eat; have you noticed that son?" The boy replied: "Yes, Papa!" Giuseppe continued. "Why do we say a prayer if the food is already in front of us?" The boy replied: "Papa because God gives us everything." Giuseppe nodded and leaned over and kissed his son's head, smiling. "Yes, my son, He gives us everything! And even if things are difficult, He gives us His friendship. So, what are we asking for in this part of the prayer, son?" "Food!" responded the boy. Giuseppe nodded. "Yes, my son, food. But when I say 'give us this day our daily bread' I think about more than food; I think about everything I need. Give me food, housing, a job, a loving family, give me my son, my daughter, and my wife and provide me with health, happiness, and peace. Even though I already have some of these, I still ask because everything comes from the Father, just as you said, son. So, when I say 'give us this day our daily bread,' I ask for what I need, but I also realize that sometimes He knows what I need more than I do. Let me give you an example, son. If you ask your mamma for lunch and she makes you a sandwich, is she giving you what you need?" The boy nodded. "Now what if you say you are hungry, and you haven't eaten anything all day! Then you say to your mother 'mamma I want a box of candy!' is candy what you need?" The boy didn't move; Giuseppe laughed. "So my son, maybe your mother knows what you need at that moment more than you know because you want a box of candy, but she knows that you need more nutrition, so she gives you a sandwich and an apple. You may complain because you didn't get candy, but you trust that your mother knows what you need. I think it is the same as the Father."

There was a silence as father and son reflected on these words. "Papa, why don't we just say, 'Always give us our daily bread?'" "Awww, excellent point, son. Why do we say 'give us this day our daily…'; why are we just asking for today and not for always? I have thought about this too, my son; can I tell you a story?" The boy smiled and clapped his hands.

"One day, a messenger arrived at the castle of a king, and he relayed this message: 'I heard from someone who heard from someone else that the neighboring kingdom is growing in wealth and strength. This person thought that you would want to know.' With these words, the messenger left."

"That night, the king went to sleep, but he kept waking up and thinking of these words 'growing in wealth and strength, growing in wealth and strength…' When he awoke, he called his guards and said, 'we have to prepare for an invasion! We have to build our walls higher; we have to ration our food; we have to train our farmers to be soldiers! Call a meeting of the people!' So, the king commanded everyone to prepare for war. Farmers abandoned their fields and trained to be soldiers, food soon ran short and had to be rationed, everyone, including women and children, had to help build the walls higher! But after the first year, the war did not come."

"The second year came, and the king said to his subjects: 'the invasion will come this year, so we have to sacrifice even more!' So, he cut the people's rations even further until children were going hungry. The crops were dead, and the people were all becoming poor. But another year went by, and still no invasion. So, it came about with the third year and then the fourth. But in the fifth year of his preparation for war, something happened. This king died suddenly. Now son, when a king dies, who becomes the next king?" "His son, Papa. But how old was his son?" Giuseppe responded, "His son was fifteen, which is still too young to rule but not too young for him to see how the people were suffering from the fear of this invasion. So, the son made a decision: he sent a delegation to the neighboring kingdom to ask the king what his intentions were. 'Are you threatening to invade our kingdom' was the question that he sent to this king."

"What happened, Papa?"

"Well, the delegation arrived, and the other king received them; instead of sending a reply, this king got on his horse and, with his guards, rode with the delegation back to the other kingdom and asked to meet with our fifteen-year-old ruler. Now the boy was nervous, and he asked his guards to make sure that no harm would come to him. The guards agreed, they all went to the grand hall, and both kings entered. The neighboring king came up to our young king, clasped his hands, and looked him in the eyes, and he said, 'I am so sorry about your father. We were like brothers when we were your age, and then we grew apart. These past five years, I have been waiting for my daughter to come of age so that I could ask him to unite our kingdoms with an alliance that would never fail, and instead, I waited too long, and he is gone. But in his memory, I extend my hand to you as a friend and an ally; I ask you to consider combining our forces'. The teenage king was surprised and blurted out, 'you mean you do not wish to invade us? You have not been planning an attack and amassing arms and men to destroy my kingdom?' The neighboring king was surprised. 'Never! I saw your father as a brother. We must set this right!' So, the two kings spoke all night and into the next day, and they drew up an alliance that both kings signed and pledged an oath of peace. This king also introduced his princess daughter to the young king, but that is another story…"

Giuseppe looked to see if the boy was following the story and then continued. "The young king returned to his room after he had signed the alliance. I wonder what he thought about those five years of sacrificing for war?" The boy looked up and thought. "He would have said that it was a waste and that his father should have given his people a better life," the boy said. Giuseppe nodded. "Yes, son. His father thought that he could control the future by sacrificing his people, but instead, he lost his own life and simply harmed his kingdom. I think it is the same with us. That is why the prayer says, 'give us this day'; we only have this day, and I can only be happy this day; yesterday, I can only remember, tomorrow I cannot yet grasp. Give me what I need this day. The people needed food, they needed to plow the fields, they needed to tend to their families, but the king forgot what they needed this day just as we sometimes do, son. When I start to worry about tomorrow, I forget about today. This part of the prayer reminds me that I am with you now, my son Joseph, my heart; if I think about my job or my bills or health or anything else, then I lose this moment, this 'dailiness' that the prayer reminds is a treasure not to be tossed out. That is why we say, 'give us this day our daily bread' because today, this moment, is more precious than any jewel."

He leaned over and kissed Joseph's head.

Forgive us our trespasses as we forgive those who trespass against us

"Papa, my friend Gio at school, told me that he was walking to his class, and an older boy started to make fun of him and wanted him to hand over his lunch money. Gio ran to class and told the teacher, but now he's scared. So is Gio supposed just to hand over his lunch money and forgive this boy?"

Giuseppe sat on his son's bed and looked into the boy's eyes a moment before answering. "Are you scared for Gio, son?" he asked. The boy nodded. "If anyone is ever mean to you at school or anywhere else, will you promise to tell me, son?" The boy nodded again.

Then Giuseppe began: "I don't think this prayer means that we have to let people walk all over us, son. But I think it has to do with what is going on in our heart," the man said, gesturing to his chest. "What do you think your friend Gio should do?" Giuseppe asked. The boy thought. "He should tell his parents and the principal at the school!" he said. Giuseppe nodded. "Yes, he doesn't have to be the victim; he can tell the adults in his life and ask them for help to make sure this doesn't happen again and also to make sure that he feels at peace at school. But I think we can consider this prayer in a bigger way, son if we back up from this situation with Gio. Let's reflect on it for a moment."

"Forgive. What does that word mean, son?" "Papa, you're supposed to know that!" the boy replied. Giuseppe smiled and said,

"Well, what does 'forgive' mean for you, son?" "Ummm, well, Emma came and got my toys and took them to her room without asking. So, I couldn't find them anywhere, and I was so mad. Then I found one toy under Emma's bed and another on the floor in her room; she didn't say anything. She didn't even say she was sorry! So, I told mamma, and she told Emma to not take my toys without asking me. So, after this…." Giuseppe intervened and asked: "What do you feel about this now, son?" The boy looked attentively at his father. "I don't think about it, Papa, but when I talk about it, I am mad!" The man patted his son's cheek. "Aww, son, that is where forgiveness comes in. As long as we don't let it go when someone harms or hurts us, we remain tied to that hurt. I don't think Emma still thinks of that day anymore. So, when you carry anger in your heart, does it hurt you or her?" "It hurts me, Papa! But she shouldn't have taken my toys…" The man nodded. "Yes, son, she shouldn't have, and your mother dealt with that. But it is difficult to be happy when we are mad, and I think our Father wants us to be happy. So, forgiveness, for me at least, is letting go of the hurt or pain and understanding that we all have our faults, that we all make mistakes and that none of us is perfect." The man looked at his son and realized that a story was in order.

"There was another king who had two sons," he began. "What is the son of a king called?" he asked. The boy responded, "A prince!" Giuseppe smiled and continued. "Like the other two princes I told you about, these had his own set of servants: secretaries, lawyers, assistants, historians, etc. These servants depended on the

Prince and the Prince on them. The secretary of one of these princes, whom we will call Prince William, approached the Prince and asked for his help. 'Your highness,' he said, 'my wife is very ill, and my children are left alone during the day. May I take leave to tend to them? The doctor says she will be ill for one year, so I have to take care of her.' Prince William saw the pain in his secretary's face and granted him leave, but the servant asked one more thing. 'Your highness, without money, I cannot buy food. Can you pay me for the year, and I will work double for you when I return to repay you?' At this, Prince William nodded, but he was also sad. 'I have not the funds to pay you for the entire year, but my brother will help. I will pay you what I can; go to him and ask for the rest. He will grant your request.' So, the man did just this. He obtained his leave of absence and his loan from both princes, and he took care of his family for the next year."

Giuseppe looked at his son and asked, "Are you sleepy, son?" The boy shook his head. Giuseppe smiled and continued. "During this time, there was a drought in the kingdom, so the crops didn't produce enough food. The king called both his sons and said, 'Sons, gather any food stored that you have and bring it to my palace; we need to ration our grain so that we can keep our people fed.' Both princes nodded and returned to their own homes."

"Now Prince William had been wise and saw signs of the drought early on. He had stored much of his crops so they could feed the people during the dry months. But his brother, who was called

Prince Michael, stored very little and was foolish to not think of the future."

"Now, do you remember the prince's secretary whose wife was ill and took a loan and a leave of absence?" The boy nodded. "Well, he returned to Prince William and told him that his wife was still sick and that he needed more time before returning to work. The Prince gave him six more months with pay. Then this same servant went to Prince Michael and made the same request, but Prince Michael's reaction was much different. 'I cannot give you more time to repay your loan,' Prince Michael screamed. 'We are short of supplies! We are short of food. I need your loan paid back in full now, or you must come and work it off, starting today!' The servant pleaded with him because of his sick wife, but the Prince wouldn't listen. So, the man went home sad; he asked his small children to take care of his wife and then began to work for Prince Michael." The boy grew indignant. "He's mean, Papa!" Giuseppe agreed.

"Are you sleepy yet, son?" he asked. Joseph again shook his head. "So, both sons went to their father, the king. Prince William was followed by cartloads of grain and wine and every type of food that he had stored; he directed them to have it transferred into his father's storerooms. Prince Michael, however, walked into his father's presence with nothing. 'Forgive me, father,' the Prince began. 'I have nothing to bring. I neglected to put food into storage when the drought began, and now, I have nothing to give you. I ask for your forgiveness'. Just then, one of the king's servants entered and whispered into the king's ear. The king looked up at his son, Prince

Michael, with pain in his face. 'I will forgive you in the same way,' he said, 'as you have forgiven the servant whose wife has taken ill.' Prince Michael frowned because he knew that he had not treated the servant with mercy as his brother had."

Giuseppe looked into his son's eyes. "Now you are sleepy, my son. But remember the story: in this prayer, we ask that we are forgiven in exactly the same way as we forgive others. Good night my son."

Lead us not into temptation

"Papa, I'm not sleepy," Joseph said as his father walked in.
Giuseppe laughed. "So, tell me," the man asked, "Which part of the
prayer comes next?" "That's easy: 'lead us not into temptation.' But
Papa, what's temptation?" Giuseppe took his son's hand and replied,
"My son, you ask me deep questions! So, let's think of this together.
What does it mean when I say that I am tempted to do something?"
The boy paused for a minute and then responded, "It's when I want
to do something that I am not supposed to do. Like taking something
that doesn't belong to me." Giuseppe nodded. "I wonder, son, if
temptation can also be *not* doing something; can I be tempted not to
do something for someone because I am too lazy or too
preoccupied?" "Yes, Papa. Sometimes we see that homeless man in
the mornings, and we don't do anything for him." "You are wise, my
son," the man said. "So, what I understand from you, son, is that
temptation can either be something I want to do, but shouldn't, or
something that I ought to do, but I don't. Do I understand you?" The
boy nodded.

"But Papa, if temptation is bad, then why would God lead us
there?" Giuseppe squeezed his son's hands. "Son, your questions are
profound, so let's think together. Do you remember when we went
camping last year, and we took that long hike in the mountains, then
I carried you down?" "Yes, Papa; we were walking so long!"
Giuseppe smiled and continued: "We went up the mountain, and we

saw an incredible view; do you remember, son? We knew that bears live in that area, so we were careful to stay on the path and keep our eyes open so that we would not lead you and Emma into harm. If we had seen a cave, we would have never led you inside because of the possibility that there could be a bear inside. Why do you think we took the safe route up that mountain, son?" "Because you didn't want anything bad to happen to us," the boy replied. "And why don't we want anything bad to happen to you, son?" Giuseppe continued. "Papa! Because you love us!" the boy said. Giuseppe nodded and leaned over and kissed his son's head. "Yes, because we love you."

"So, if I, your father, watch out for you and try to keep you from danger, wouldn't the Father in heaven do the same, and more?" he asked. "Yes, Papa, so why do we ask him not to lead us into temptation, then?" "Yes, son. You didn't need to ask me to avoid that cave; I wouldn't have brought you there whether you asked me or not, because I love you. So why do we ask the Father not to lead us into the cave of temptation? Would He lead us there if we didn't ask? I don't think so; He is the Father. For me, son, in the words of this prayer, I am simply thanking the Father for always watching out for us. As a grown man someday, it would be like you came to me and said, 'Papa, thank you for always trying to protect me.' You are recognizing and thanking me for doing what I would do anyway because I love you. So, when I say these words of that prayer, I am thinking about how grateful I am to have a Father who always watches out for me and takes care of me and those I love. Does that make sense, my son?" The boy nodded as Giuseppe started to get up. "Wait, Papa!" the boy said, and the man sat back down.

"Papa, you forgot a word!" Giuseppe looked perplexed. "Lead!" the boy said. Giuseppe looked up in thought and then met eyes with the boy. "If there is a leader, then there must be a follower, right, son? So, who is leading me? Well, I have choices. I can lead myself and follow no one, or I can organize my life around someone that I admire or love; I can be part of a group of people and adopt what they think and do, or I can follow an idea or political party and base my life on that. You see, son, each one of us can decide how to lead our lives and who to follow or not follow. Now, if I look at my own life, son, there were times when I wanted to be in charge, and I didn't want anyone telling me what to do, including the Father." "Why, Papa?" the boy asked. "Well, if I am honest, it felt better to trust myself than someone else. But then a series of things happened that helped me realize that I cannot control everything: I cannot control when someone I care about gets sick or even dies; I cannot control when and with whom I would fall in love, I cannot control other people, I cannot control many things. Son, in this part of the prayer, when I ask the Father to lead me, I ask him to help me to cooperate with him instead of ignoring him. Does that make sense, son?" he asked. Joseph did not reply, so Giuseppe continued.

"There was another kingdom in another land far away, and this king had two daughters, Princess Elizabeth and Princess Caterina. Both loved their father and mother, the queen and king, intensely, and though he had no sons, the king was proud of his daughters, and the people loved the royal family. Both of these princesses wanted to do good for the kingdom, so Princess Elizabeth went to her father every morning with the request: 'Father, what would you have me do for you today?' The king would give her some instructions which she would carry out. Princess Caterina, on the other hand, was more independent-minded. Rather than ask her father what he wanted her to do, she would ask him what he wanted for his people once a year and what kind of a kingdom he wanted for his lands. Then, this princess went out to be with people every day and to carry out what she understood her father's vision was. For example, her father wanted the people in his kingdom to help one another and not be selfish with what they had. Princess Caterina helped organize the people so that nobody would go hungry, nobody be lonely, and everyone would feel like they mattered both to the king and to one another."

"Now Princess Elizabeth rarely left the palace for she was busy carrying out her father's orders every day. She was careful not to show anger or impatience because she understood that she had a responsibility to be the perfect daughter since her father was the king."

"Princess Caterina, on the other hand, worked with the people every day and got her hands dirty. She helped serve meals, build walls, and provide housing. She sometimes showed impatience, but the people overlooked this since she had a good heart."

"Now, son, both Princess Elizabeth and Caterina did the will of their father. Elizabeth was her father's servant, always obeying his will, whereas Caterina saw herself as her father's companion, cooperating with his will in ways that she understood. The one was perfect but stayed in the palace's safety, the other was imperfect but helped transform the kingdom. If you were king, which daughter would please you more?" "I like Caterina more!" the boy said. "Why, son?" Giuseppe asked. "Because she didn't act like a slave, she acted like the king's daughter" was the response. "Yes, son, and that is exactly how it is with the Father and us. When we ask to be led by the Father, it is not as slaves but as sons and daughters, just like Caterina. Good night my son," he said as he kissed the boy.

Deliver us from evil

"We are almost finished discussing our prayer, my son," Giuseppe began as he entered the room and sat on the bed. "I am learning a lot from our discussions, too, and I am happy. Are you happy, my son?" The boy nodded, and Giuseppe smiled. "Tell me the next part of the prayer, my son," he continued. The boy recited, "'Deliver us from evil.' But Papa, what does it mean to deliver?" Giuseppe responded, "My son, with the deep questions! What does it mean to deliver...for me it means to save us from evil, not let us fall into evil…" "But what's evil, then?" the boy interrupted. "Let's think about that, my son," the man replied.

"Papa, does it mean that, if I am good, God won't let anything bad happen to me?" the boy asked. Giuseppe began: "Remember son, the Father is not Santa Claus. Sometimes good and bad happen to all of us; I think the difference is that the Father will not abandon us; he will always be your friend, son. If He doesn't always shield us from challenges and difficulties, son, what are we asking the Father to deliver us from?" The boy squinted. "I don't know, Papa." "That's fine, son. Let's reflect together."

"What helps me, son, is when I think of what I want you to be delivered from. I want you to be delivered from sadness, from loneliness, from ignorance, from a pointless life. I want you to be happy and feel like you belong; I want you to be knowledgeable and to know that you matter so much, that you are so precious to your mother and me and all of us. So, if I don't want you to be sad, how much more the Father. And if I don't want you to feel lonely, or to be ignorant or to have a life without meaning, so much more the Father. So, when I say the words 'deliver us from evil' I ask the Father for you and me and everyone that we may be delivered from these things."

"Remember son, that when we say these words we keep saying 'our,' 'us,' 'we'; that is because, when we ask the Father for His help, He is the Father of all of us, so I ask not just for myself but for all His sons and daughters. When I ask Him that He may deliver me from the evil of sadness and ignorance, I ask this for you and my neighbor and that homeless man down the street. When I ask to be delivered from living a pointless life, I ask for myself and those who struggle to discover why they have been placed here. When I pray that I will be saved from loneliness, I also ask for my coworkers and those whose names I don't know, even those I pass on the freeway, that we might recognize our kinship with one Father. I ask to be delivered from my distractions so that I see what is important and cooperate with the Father. So, for me, son, evil is not first of all what might happen to me out there in the world but is what I allow to live in my heart…"

The man looked at his son and realized that he needed another story. "A poor family was living in a kingdom many years ago," he began. "This man worked the fields on his lord's estate and had a small house with a dirt floor, only one room, his wife, and four children." "That's too small, Papa!" the boy interjected. Giuseppe agreed. "It was small, but this man, John, was grateful for the little he had. Now he had three sons and one daughter; each one's personality was so different. John sometimes remarked to Maria, his wife, that they seemed to come from four different sets of parents! The oldest boy, Jonathan, was talkative and always asking questions. The second oldest, James, was quiet and shy but was interested in learning about plants and animals. The third child, the daughter, loved to be close to her mother all day long; her name was Cecilia; and the fourth child, a boy like you, liked to play games for hours, either with his brothers and sister or with the farm animals." Giuseppe looked to make sure that Joseph was still awake. "Shall I continue, son?" The boy nodded.

"Now one day, a storyteller arrived in this land, and he spun tales of far off adventures, of dragons and knights and heroes. Jonathan and James heard these stories and got it into their heads that they would leave their father's house to seek out these adventures when they came of age. When the day arrived that they were leaving, their parents were sad; the boys promised to return soon and tell them everything they would encounter and experience. So, they left and did not return for two years!" "That's a long time, Papa," the boy added. Giuseppe nodded.

"The day the boys did return, their parents noticed that they were different. Jonathan, who had always been talkative and an adventurer, was quiet and withdrawn, and James, how had been shy, now was bubbling over with the stories. Each boy had experienced the same hardships and challenges, yet it affected them in different ways. As the days and weeks passed, John grew concerned about Jonathan, who was not the same boy as before. 'How was your adventure, son?' he asked. The boy was quiet. 'Did somebody hurt you, son?' he continued. The boy didn't respond. 'Tell me what is in your heart, son,' the man urged. At this, Jonathan looked up and said, 'I left for adventure, but I found loneliness and despair. I was afraid and ashamed to be afraid. I felt that I didn't belong anywhere, that nothing I did mattered to anyone, while James had no fear. I'm sorry, Papa,' he said. The man looked at his son with compassion and said, "I am sorry you have suffered so much. You are never alone; I carried you in my heart every day that you were gone, as I do now. And you matter to me above all else; I just wasn't close by so that I could remind you. And as far as being scared, we all get scared, son. I was so frightened when your mother brought you into this world, wondering if I would be a good father if I could protect you from harm, I wondered if I could help you grow to be the man you are destined to be. And you are growing into that man, son. I was so frightened when you left two years ago. I am sorry that the evil of despair made its way into your heart and made you forget that you are not alone, that you matter, that you are loved and that you are perfect."

Giuseppe stopped and looked at his son, who was yawning. "And I think it is the same between the Father and us," he concluded. "Good night, son," he said, kissing the boy's head.

Amen

"Hi Papa, Hi Mamma!" the boy cried out as both parents came in to wish him goodnight. "Did you enjoy your father's explanations of the prayer?" Helen asked, putting her hand on Giuseppe's shoulder, who was sitting on the bed. "Yes, Mamma, but we are not finished!" Giuseppe and Helen looked perplexed. "Papa, you forgot the last part! What does 'Amen' mean?" Both parents smiled. "I'm going to let you two finish up now while I put Emma to bed," she said as she bent down and kissed the boy on the forehead. "Good night, Mamma," he said. "I love you, son," Helen said as she left.

"All these evenings reflecting on the prayer has helped me also, son," Giuseppe said. "Now, when we say the *Our Father,* we have much to think about," he added.

"So, Papa..." the boy began. "I know, son," he said, looking into the boy's eyes. "What does it mean to say 'amen,' no?" Joseph nodded. "Well, for me, when I say 'amen' I am saying that I agree, I accept what is being said into my heart. So, if you say a prayer and I listen to you, son, and if, in the end, I say 'amen,' then your prayer becomes mine also. If I say a prayer and conclude by saying 'amen,' I am saying that I agree with every part of that prayer that I just said. A group of people can also say 'amen' together if they accept the prayer that has been said..."

"So, Papa, 'amen' means 'I agree;' so if Emma tells me something true, I can say 'amen'?" "You can say that, my son, but mostly that word is used when you are finishing praying. It doesn't only mean that you agree; it means that you agree and accept it in your heart. There is a difference. When I hear you say your prayers, son, I always say 'amen' because I want your prayer to be in my heart. It is much more than agreeing; I want those words to become part of me. That is what 'amen' means to me."

"Son, with all these things we have reflected on, why don't you say the *Our Father* now, and I will agree with all my heart." The boy nodded and began.

Other titles from Higher Ground Books & Media:

Wise Up to Rise Up by Rebecca Benston

A Path to Shalom by Steen Burke

For His Eyes Only by John Salmon, Ph.D.

Miracles: I Love Them by Forest Godin

32 Days with Christ's Passion by Mark Etter

Knowing Affliction and Doing Recovery by John Baldasare

Out of Darkness by Stephen Bowman

Breaking the Cycle by Willie Deeanjlo White

Healing in God's Power by Yvonne Green

Chronicles of a Spiritual Journey by Stephen Shepherd

The Real Prison Diaries by Judy Frisby

My Name is Sam...And Heaven is Still Shining Through by Joe Siccardi

Add these titles to your collection today!

http://www.highergroundbooksandmedia.com

Do you have a story to tell?

Higher Ground Books & Media is an independent Christian-based publisher specializing in stories of triumph! Our purpose is to empower, inspire, and educate through the sharing of personal experiences.

Please visit our website for our submission guidelines.

http://www.highergroundbooksandmedia.com

Made in the USA
Middletown, DE
17 November 2021

52735175R00033